JAY LENO
IF ROAST BEEF COULD FLY

Illustrated by S. B. WHITEHEAD

A Byron Preiss Visual Publications, Inc. Book

SIMON & SCHUSTER BOOKS FOR YOUNG READERS
New York   London   Toronto   Sydney

When my dad decides to make something, he always calls it a "project." Fixing the car is a "project." Cleaning the gutters is a "project."

"I'm ready for my next project," he tells me one spring day. This means he has finished the winter "car project," even though there's a lot left to do on it.

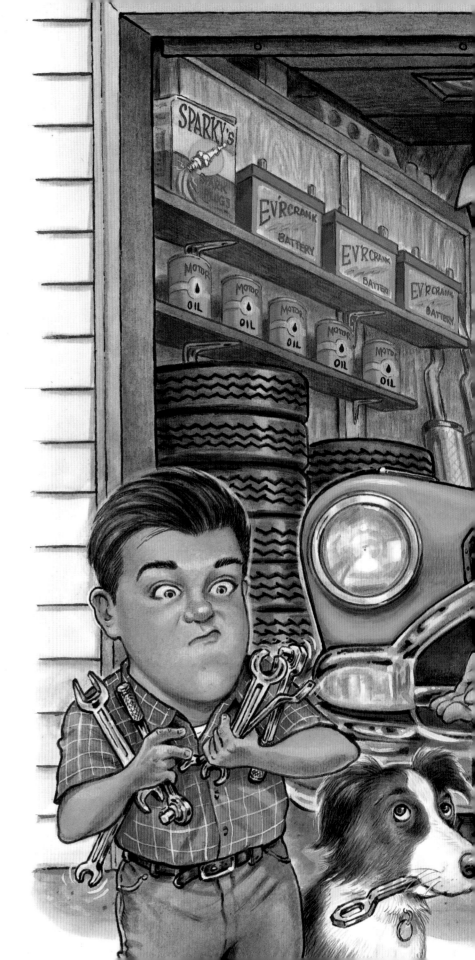

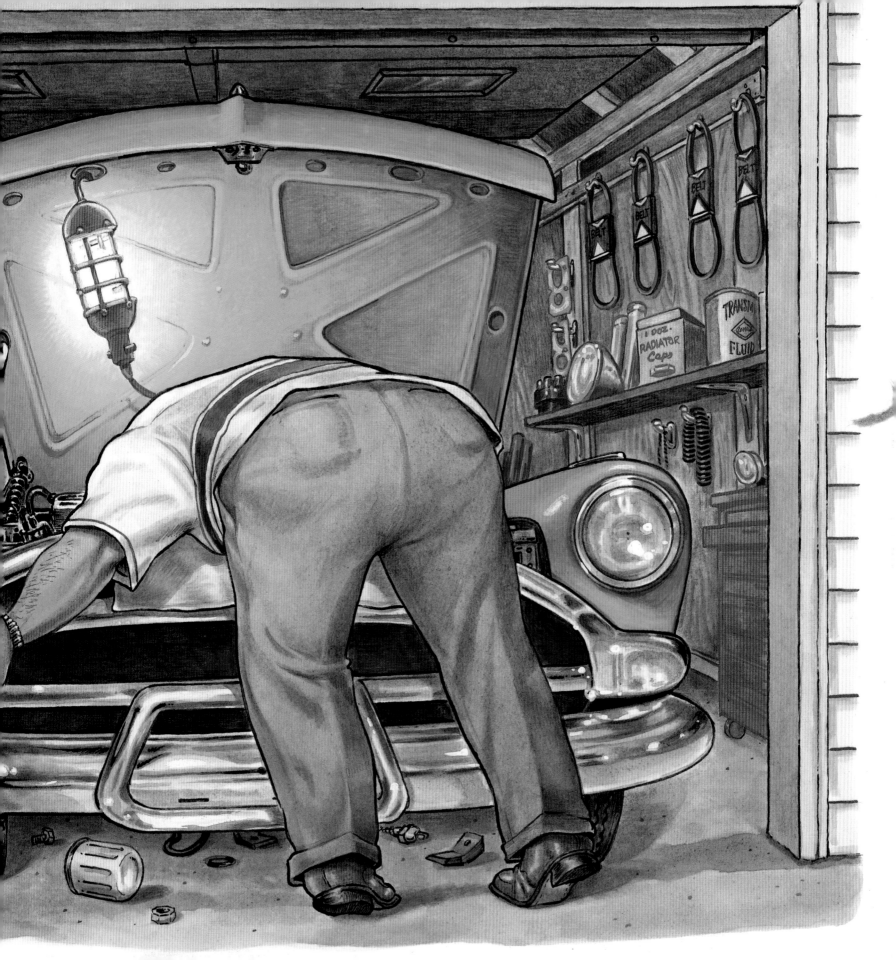

The great thing about working with my dad is he loves taking things apart. . . . He just doesn't get around to putting them back together!

"This summer we're going to have ourselves the greatest barbecue ever!" Dad announces. "No more charcoal! No more lighter fluid! We're going to build a patio deck and get us a rotisserie!"

I smile. I have no idea what a rotisserie is, but Dad sure is excited.

"Come on, son! Grab Bruce! Let's go to the Hardware Supermax store!"

The little hardware store in town was never good enough for the projects Dad wanted to do. No, we had to drive sixty miles to a giant superstore 'cause everything my dad and his side of the family did was BIG . . . even dinner!

My dad's side of the family is Italian. Every Sunday we have four hundred pounds of meatballs, half a ton of spaghetti, a swimming pool's worth of sauce!

Okay, maybe I exaggerate, but compared to my mom's side of the family, my dad's side is extravagant! My mom's side of the family is Scottish and thrifty. They like to save everything.

When I visit my mom's sister, Aunt Nettie, she makes me her idea of a great snack—it's a can of warm soda and a dry biscuit called a "scone."

She keeps the soda in the cupboard because, in her mind, to refrigerate even one can would somehow quadruple the cost of electricity! When she opens the can for me, there's always a long wheezing *sssss*. "Mmmmmm!" I say to myself. "Flat, warm cola!"

For my dad everything had to be the biggest and the best. That's why when we get to the store, Dad starts giving orders to everybody.

"Okay! We need five hundred bricks! Two hundred pounds of cement! Son, you tell the clerk about the rotisserie equipment!"

"We want the biggest, most expensive rotisserie ever made," I say to the clerk. I still don't know exactly what a rotisserie is, but I knew I wanted the best, just like Dad.

Dad and I couldn't fit everything we bought into the car for the ride home, but the Hardware Supermax guys said they would give us free delivery. In fact, they said they would follow us home.

Dad is very proud that we have everything we need for the project. Unfortunately, when Dad does a project, he always winds up making more work for everybody else . . . especially Mom.

When we drive up, Mom and Aunt Nettie shake their heads in unison.

"Oh, the waste," they sigh. "The waste!"

The delivery crew finally unloads everything. Bruce tries to help by barking at the truck's tires.

This is what it must have been like to watch the building of the pyramids of Egypt! I hope our patio won't take five hundred years.

Pretty soon the whole neighborhood gathers in our backyard. Experts are consulted. In my neighborhood everyone is an expert. I'm sure the patio will take twice as long to build if Dad listens to everybody's advice!

Weeks later we are just about finished with the patio, except for the lights, the storm drain, the fence, and the steps to the backyard. We do, however, have a really neat dirt path. I realize the summer is almost over and we haven't had our first barbecue yet.

"Don't worry, son," says Dad. "We're going to have the best end-of-summer barbecue ever!"

Mom and Aunt Nettie deliver the invitations by hand. No need to waste envelopes and stamps.

At last the night of the big party arrives. In my mom's eyes, if there is anything worse than wasting money, it is showing off, which is something my dad and I love to do.

What better way to show off than by making a grand entrance into the party? Ta-daaa!

Unfortunately I do not realize the banister is so steep.

I begin to pick up speed at a tremendous rate.

FOOF!

It's a good thing we bought too much cement!

Dad is in too good a mood to let my little stunt bother him. He helps me up and smiles. "Look!"

There are Aunt Nettie and Mom bringing out the biggest roast beef I've ever seen. Bruce is jumping up and down in his awkward way, like a rag doll on a trampoline.

The neighbors fall silent. Dad flicks the switch on the rotisserie. So that's how it works! In less than a heartbeat the roast beef begins to turn on the spit. *"Ooooh! Ahhhh!"* Everybody watches the meat roasting.

Dad goes inside to help Mom serve the several different tons of food brought by Dad's family. I'm all alone with the roast beef. Boy, does it smell good.

For me this spinning roast beef is an amazing spectacle. Juice is dripping! Fat is sizzling! The spit is making little metallic *eee-eee* noises as it turns. I can't take my eyes off it. I'm dying to taste the roast beef. But how can I do it without anyone knowing?

Then I get an idea.*

I reach deep into my pocket. I pull out my secret weapon. It is just long enough to reach the top of the meat in the rotisserie.

*Kids, don't try this at home!

I stick it into the turning roast beef and get a little bit. Delicious!

I look around the patio. Everybody else is inside waiting for Dad to tell them the meat is ready. I do it over and over again! Instant roast beef!

Then the worst thing happens.

My secret weapon gets stuck in the string that Mom has tied around the roast beef to keep it on the spit! I can't pull it loose. The roast beef keeps turning. I have to let go of the weapon. It's slowly melting into the roast beef! I don't know what to do!

Suddenly Dad decides it's time to bring the roast beef inside. The backyard is dark. Everybody is hungry, even Aunt Nettie. We all sit down to watch Dad carve.

"Oh, boy!" he shouts. "A new patio! A new rotisserie! A beautiful day!"

Dad starts to slice the roast beef . . .

He can't cut the meat! The dining room is silent except for the sound of the knife. It sounds like Dad is sawing wood, but I know it isn't wood, it's . . .

"plastic!"

Dad shouts.

A big chunk of my comb falls on the plate and goes *clank!* The meat underneath it is all pink. Dad starts breathing hard like he's going to explode.

"What the heck is this?!" he bellows.

Very quietly I whisper, "Oh . . . um . . . it's my secret weapon."

"What's your secret weapon?" he roars.

"It's my comb," I say.

"Your comb?"

Dad picks up the roast beef like a football and throws it out the window. Everybody is just standing there, mouths open, stunned . . . or maybe just hungry.

"Look!" shouts Aunt Nettie as the roast beef sails through the air. Out of nowhere, as if in slow motion, as graceful as LeBron James going up for a rebound, Bruce leaps across the sky and catches the roast beef, gently cradling it in his jaws before gliding back to earth.

"That dog never caught anything in his life," he says, undefeated. "Everybody! Listen! Inside the house we have more than four hundred pounds of cole slaw, eight tons of macaroni, and all the salad you can eat!"

As everybody finishes the main course of potato salad, Dad gets that old "project" gleam in his eyes. He's looking at the rest of the backyard.

"I have our next project, son!" he says. "We have all this cement left over. . . . What do you think about . . .

"... a swimming pool?"

I see Bruce starting to dig the hole already.

To my mom and dad, and

to my brother and

my aunts and uncles and cousins,

all of whom made my

childhood so safe and

so much fun

—J. L.

SIMON & SCHUSTER BOOKS FOR YOUNG READERS

An imprint of Simon & Schuster Children's Publishing Division

1230 Avenue of the Americas, New York, New York 10020

Book design by Arnie Sawyer

Special thanks to Helga Pollock.

The text for this book is set in Breugel.

The illustrations for this book are rendered in watercolor.

Manufactured in the United States of America

2 4 6 8 10 9 7 5 3

CIP data for this book is available from the Library of Congress.

ISBN 0-689-86767-0